D0819898

The Magical Guide to the
WIZARDING WORLD

Written by Elizabeth Dowsett,
Julia March, and Rosie Peet

CONTENTS

INTRODUCTION

Welcome to the spellbinding world of LEGO® Harry Potter™! Get ready to explore these magical LEGO Harry Potter sets inspired by the Harry Potter films. Ride the Hogwarts Express, visit Hogwarts Castle, open up the Great Hall, and see the Whomping Willow at work. If you're feeling brave, you can even take a peek inside Aragog's Lair!

You'll meet a whole host of LEGO Harry Potter minifigures, too. Harry, Ron, and Hermione are all here. So are their friends and foes, including animal companions, teachers, and classmates from all four Hogwarts houses.

Turn the page ... and let the magic begin!

WELCOME TO HOGWARTS

Hogwarts School of Witchcraft and Wizardry is a school
like no other. Young witches and wizards come here
to learn magical skills and make friends for life.
The castle is impossible for nonmagical people to find,
so it is a safe place for young students to practice
their magical skills.

HOGWARTS EXPRESS

A **magical** scarlet **steam train** that transports students to and from **Hogwarts**.

*E*very September 1st at 11am, the Hogwarts Express leaves London to carry young wizards and witches to Hogsmeade Station for the new school year at Hogwarts School of Witchcraft and Wizardry.

In the LEGO® Hogwarts Express set, the gleaming red steam engine, a coal car, and a passenger carriage pull into King's Cross Station. Minifigures cross the tracks using an arched railroad bridge. On the bridge, a clock with movable hands counts the minutes until 11am. Once on platform 9, there is one more thing minifigures must do to board the train. They run straight at a special section of wall, where a block of LEGO bricks pivots to open a door to platform 9¾—a secret platform magically hidden from Muggles.

LEGO set: Hogwarts™ Express (75955)

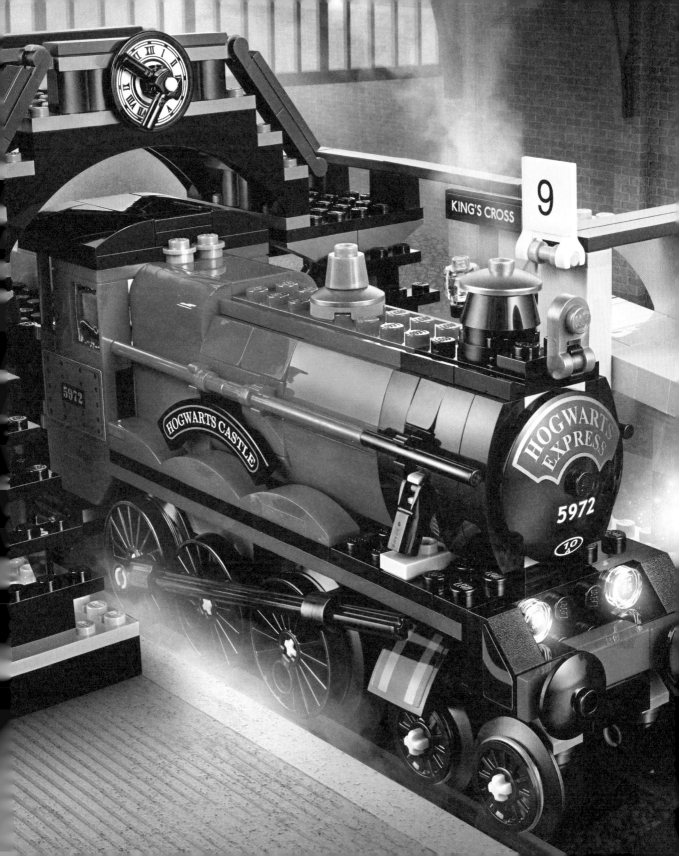

HARRY POTTER

The **Boy Who Lived** and **Hogwarts'** most **famous** student.

R aised by his Muggle aunt and uncle, Harry was 11 before he learned that he was a wizard and was invited to study at Hogwarts School of Witchcraft and Wizardry.

In this LEGO set, the Harry minifigure is off to begin a new term at school. He waits at London's King's Cross Station, ready to board the Hogwarts Express. Standing on short, nonposeable legs, Harry has come wearing plain gray pants and a blue zipped jacket. Students never wear their wizarding robes in public!

Behind Harry is a stand selling copies of the *Daily Prophet* newspaper. Today, the front-page story is about "The Boy Who Lived." That's Harry himself! He got that name after a close scrape with a powerful Dark wizard.

House: Gryffindor **Patronus:** Stag **Animal companion**: Hedwig the owl
LEGO set: Hogwarts™ Express (75955), Aragog's Lair (75950)

HERMIONE GRANGER

The **brightest** witch of her age and a **brave, loyal** friend.

*F*iercely intelligent Hermione Granger grew up in the Muggle world with her dentist parents. She is about to start a new term at Hogwarts School of Witchcraft and Wizardry. Here she will learn new spells, brew incredible potions, and meet amazing magical creatures!

In this LEGO set, the Hermione minifigure rushes over the railroad bridge as fast as her short, nonposable legs will carry her. She wears a casual, striped hoodie that's unique to the Hogwarts Express set. She clutches her luggage and her wand, ready for the year ahead at school. On the other side of the bridge is the concealed entrance to platform 9¾, where Hermione will board the Hogwarts Express with her fellow students.

House: Gryffindor **Patronus:** Otter **Animal Companion:** Crookshanks the cat **LEGO set:** Hogwarts™ Express (75955)

RON WEASLEY

A **cheerful** wizard and a good friend with **hidden heroic** qualities.

Friendly Ron Weasley is the sixth boy in his family to go to Hogwarts. Like all Weasleys, Ron has red hair, but he also has a special sense of humor that's all his own.

The Weasley family is large and loving but not very rich, so Ron usually ends up with a lot of hand-me-downs. This Ron minifigure, from the LEGO Harry Potter Hogwarts Express set, is dressed in his brother Bill's old plaid jacket. He pushes a LEGO luggage cart filled with second-hand items from family members. Ron's luggage includes Percy's old rat, Scabbers, and Charlie's cast-off wand.

With his cheery, freckled face, Ron made friends with Harry after helping him get through the magical barrier to platform 9¾. The two have been best friends ever since.

House: Gryffindor **Patronus:** Jack Russell **Animal Companion:** Scabbers the rat **LEGO sets:** Hogwarts™ Express (75955), Aragog's Lair (75950)

JOURNEY TO HOGWARTS

Travel to school in style with tasty treats!

Your carriage awaits in the LEGO Hogwarts Express. Aboard the train, Hogwarts students settle down to share all the latest news. Ron and Harry are in a four-seat train car, which has a removable side-panel and roof. Beside Ron is Scabbers the rat, who remains beige despite Ron's efforts to bewitch his fur yellow. Each minifigure has a comfy chair to relax in while the countryside flies by.

Here comes the Trolley Witch with a cart full of snacks. The witch minifigure sells magical treats such as Chocolate Frogs and Bertie Bott's Every-Flavour Beans. It's a good thing the LEGO train car has closed windows, so Ron's Chocolate Frog can't hop out of one!

LEGO set: Hogwarts™ Express (75955)

FIRST GLIMPSE OF HOGWARTS

A lantern-lit **boat trip** across the **lake** to school.

The final part of the journey to Hogwarts is a moonlit boat trip across a lake.

In the LEGO Hogwarts Great Hall set, the Ron, Harry, Hermione, and Susan Bones minifigures share a boat. A lantern hangs at the prow to light their way in the dark. They are all dressed in their Hogwarts school uniforms. Hagrid, Keeper of Keys and Grounds at Hogwarts, waits on the jetty holding a lantern. Professor McGonagall and Professor Dumbledore stand ready to greet the students. This Dumbledore minifigure, in dark red robes, is unique to this set. Hogwarts' huge front doors can be swung open to reveal the Great Hall.

LEGO set: Hogwarts™ Great Hall (75954)

SORTING HAT

A **thinking cap** that can see into your **head!**

This battered old hat may not look impressive, but it carries the intelligence of the four founding wizards and witches of Hogwarts. The smart Sorting Hat looks into the students' minds in order to place them in the house best suited to them. It can also talk, sing, and give advice!

In the Hogwarts Great Hall set, a Professor McGonagall minifigure stands ready to place the Sorting Hat on the head of each new student. It's all part of the Sorting Ceremony that takes place at the start of each year. The table behind McGonagall has a goblet laid out for the welcoming feast. It's Susan Bones's turn to swap her LEGO hairpiece for the Hat. And the verdict is ... Hufflepuff!

LEGO set: Hogwarts™ Great Hall (75954)

GODRIC GRYFFINDOR

The founder of **Gryffindor house** and a **courageous** leader.

Godric Gryffindor was one of the four founders of Hogwarts. Godric valued bravery and determination. He thrived in battle and was talented at dueling. He believed that Muggle-born witches and wizards should be allowed to attend Hogwarts. His fellow Hogwarts founder, Salazar Slytherin, did not agree.

In the LEGO Hogwarts Castle set, Godric wears medieval wizard robes in vivid scarlet and gold, the colors of Gryffindor house. His red hair and bushy beard resemble a lion's mane. He wields a wand in one hand and the Sword of Gryffindor in the other. Harry uses this ancient sword to fight the Basilisk in the Chamber of Secrets during his second year at Hogwarts.

House: Gryffindor **Skills:** Dueling **Characteristics:** Courage, bravery, and determination **LEGO set:** Hogwarts™ Castle (71043)

SALAZAR SLYTHERIN

The Hogwarts **founder** who judged people **by their ancestry.**

O ne of the four great founders of Hogwarts, Salazar Slytherin believed that only students from pure-blood wizarding families should be allowed in. This caused a rift between him and the other founders of Hogwarts.

Exclusive to the LEGO Hogwarts Castle set, the Slytherin minifigure wears green and silver robes printed with snakelike patterns. His stern face is partly covered by a long, white beard that falls in serpentine shapes. Around Slytherin's neck hangs a locket engraved with "S," which he has enchanted so that only a Parselmouth like himself can open it. A Parselmouth is someone who can speak the language of snakes. What secrets might the locket conceal?

House: Slytherin **Skills:** Parselmouth **Characteristics:** Cunning, pride, ambition **LEGO set:** Hogwarts™ Castle (71043)

HELGA HUFFLEPUFF

The Hogwarts founder who **embodied fairness and equality**.

Helga Hufflepuff didn't distinguish between students in the way her fellow founders did. Anyone was welcome in her house, but she encouraged them to work hard and treat everyone justly.

In the LEGO Hogwarts Castle set, the Helga minifigure has long, braided hair piled up on her head. She is dressed in unshowy brown robes. The back of her bodice has a laced-up print hidden under her cloak. Hufflepuff house's badger symbol is printed on her belt and the clasp of her cloak. She holds a golden cup, now a relic known as Hufflepuff's cup, in one hand and her wand in the other.

House: Hufflepuff **Skills:** Charms, cookery **Characteristics:** Dedication, patience, loyalty **LEGO set:** Hogwarts™ Castle (71043)

ROWENA RAVENCLAW

The most brilliant witch of her era and a founder of Hogwarts.

Ravenclaw house takes its name from the brilliant Rowena Ravenclaw. Known for her sharp and curious mind, Ravenclaw believed that "wit beyond measure is man's greatest treasure." She wanted to teach the brightest young witches and wizards at Hogwarts.

Rowena Ravenclaw wears long, blue robes with a skirt piece. Blue became the Ravenclaw house color and is seen, along with the symbol of the eagle, on the house banner.

The Rowena minifigure's dress is decorated with metallic printing that echoes the night sky—just like the ceiling in the Ravenclaw common room. Her eagle diadem (crown) sits on her forehead, above her smiling face.

House: Ravenclaw **Skills:** Problem solving **Characteristics:** Wit, learning, wisdom **LEGO set:** Hogwarts™ Castle (71043)

TEACHERS

The teachers at Hogwarts live in the castle just like the students. They are an interesting bunch! Professor Dumbledore, the wise headmaster, is known for his love of sherbet lemon candies. Stern Professor McGonagall is an eager Quidditch fan. Hagrid, the gamekeeper, is a gentle soul with a fondness for dangerous creatures.

PROFESSOR DUMBLEDORE

Hogwarts **headmaster** and the **greatest wizard** of them all.

*A*lbus Percival Wulfric Brian Dumbledore is one of the most powerful wizards in the wizarding world, and the headmaster of Hogwarts. He inspires loyalty and respect. Dumbledore's list of achievements is longer than his flowing white beard, and it's said he is the only person that Lord Voldemort fears.

Despite his important position, Dumbledore has a light-hearted side. There is often a twinkle in his eye, behind his half-moon glasses. His minifigure, in pale-blue silk robes and a cap with a golden tassel, carries the first-ever LEGO® Pensieve. This enchanted shallow stone dish holds swirling memories. It conjures up very real and vivid scenes. Those who look into the Pensieve see memories as if they themselves were there at the time.

House: Gryffindor **Patronus:** Phoenix **Favorite candy:** Sherbet lemons
LEGO set: LEGO® Minifigures (71022)

PROFESSOR MCGONAGALL

A strict but fair teacher, and the respected head of Gryffindor house.

Minerva McGonagall has taught at Hogwarts for years. She teaches Transfiguration, the art of turning one object into another. She is also head of Gryffindor house. However, Gryffindor students don't get any special treatment from this fair-minded teacher.

Every year, Professor McGonagall presides over the Sorting Ceremony in the Great Hall. She welcomes the year's new arrivals with a wave of her wand. Her minifigure wears a traditional pointed witch's hat and dark-green robes. Although she has a reputation for being strict, McGonagall's warm, friendly expression is likely to reassure nervous first-year students.

House: Gryffindor **Subject:** Transfiguration **Animagus:** Tabby cat
LEGO set: Hogwarts™ Great Hall (75954)

PROFESSOR FLITWICK

The **part-goblin** Charms professor and **Head of Ravenclaw** house.

*F*ilius Flitwick is the beloved and respected Charms teacher. Generations of witches and wizards have benefited from his patient and caring teaching style—and occasionally witnessed his mischievous streak.

Flitwick's goblin-sized minifigure has short, nonposeable legs and a cheerful face printed with bushy eyebrows, a mustache, and silver glasses. He wears his Yule Ball outfit, a dashing suit with tails made of LEGO cape fabric. A bow tie sits between the head and torso pieces.

Although Flitwick leads the Hogwarts choir and orchestra, his squeaky voice is far from musical. He has to use a megaphone to be heard above the crowd!

House: Ravenclaw **Subject:** Charms **Characteristics:** Humor, intelligence, bravery **LEGO set:** LEGO® Minifigures (71022)

MADAM HOOCH

Strict flying teacher, keen broom expert, and eagle-eyed Quidditch referee.

Rolanda Hooch is the flying instructor and Quidditch referee at Hogwarts. This sharp-tongued teacher is both feared and respected by her students. She is well known for being a fair but firm referee. She does not tolerate any cheating or funny business. When she barks out orders, she expects obedience—or else!

This Madam Hooch LEGO minifigure is dressed to referee a Quidditch match. She has her flying cape on and the jacket printed on her torso is pinned closed so that it doesn't flap around while airborne. Turn her double-sided head to see she's fastened on her flying goggles! Hooch is an expert on what makes a good broom. Her own broom is kept neatly trimmed, just like her windswept gray hair!

Hobbies: Broomstick enthusiast **First broomstick:** Silver Arrow
Skill: Flying **LEGO set:** LEGO® Harry Potter™ Exclusive Set (5005254)

PROFESSOR SNAPE

Hogwarts' **stern,** secretive, and clever **Potions master.**

*S*everus Snape is the mysterious Head of Slytherin house. He teaches Potions in his dungeon classroom. This sarcastic Professor is stern with Harry from the moment they meet. With his cross expression and sweeping dark robes, Professor Snape could strike fear into the heart of even the bravest Gryffindor.

In the Hogwarts Whomping Willow set, Snape sits in his gloomy office. On the wall behind him hangs a portrait. His potion bottles are stored neatly away on shelves. Snape has taken a break from grading homework with his feather quill to read the *Daily Prophet*. His least-favorite student, Harry, is on the front page. Perhaps that's why Snape's minifigure face is frowning!

House: Slytherin **Subject:** Potions **Patronus:** Doe **LEGO sets:** Hogwarts™ Whomping Willow™ (75953), Quidditch™ Match (75956)

RUBEUS HAGRID

The **gamekeeper** at Hogwarts and a friend to **dangerous creatures.**

With his untamed hair and beard, Rubeus Hagrid looks like he has wrestled with one of the wild, magical creatures he cares for! Hagrid may look daunting, but he has a heart of gold. He is always kind to those in need, including dangerous animals such as dragons and giant spiders!

Hagrid's oversized LEGO minifigure reflects his half-giant origins. He wears robes with a giant belt buckle and a huge moleskin overcoat. He also carries a pink umbrella, said to conceal an illegal wand (he is banned from doing magic since being expelled from Hogwarts). Hagrid works as gamekeeper at the school and, from Harry's third year, as the Care of Magical Creatures teacher.

House: Gryffindor **Subject:** Care of Magical Creatures
Skills: Raising dragons **LEGO set:** Hogwarts™ Great Hall (75954)

PROFESSOR TRELAWNEY

The eccentric **Divination** teacher who believes she can **predict the future.**

Sybill Trelawney teaches Divination, the art of predicting the future. She is the great-great-granddaughter of a famous "Seer"—a witch who could see into the future. However, many people think Sybill makes up her predictions!

The absentminded professor can normally be found in her cluttered classroom at the top of the Divination Tower. Her LEGO minifigure wears oversized glasses; amulets around her neck; and a scarf tied over her wild, unruly hair. Trelawney's bohemian robes are printed with patterns, layers, and tassels. Sybill comes with a teacup, too. Well, you never know when she might want to read the future in her tea leaves.

House: Ravenclaw **Subject:** Divination **Hobbies:** Reading tea leaves, crystal ball gazing **LEGO set:** LEGO® Minifigures (71022)

PROFESSOR SLUGHORN

Potions professor and admirer of wealth and power.

Do you have what it takes to join the Slug Club? This exclusive group is chosen by the Potions professor, Horace Slughorn. Only the brightest students can expect an invitation to his Slug Club gatherings. It helps to be from an important family, too! The pompous professor is charming and helpful to rich, powerful, or clever people. Students he doesn't rate highly are ignored.

Slughorn's LEGO minifigure is dressed in tweed with a printed waistcoat and bow tie. His gray hair piece has a side part. He carries a vial of green potion expertly brewed in his dungeon classroom. Could it be a prize for the student who brews the best potion in class?

House: Slytherin **Subject:** Potions **Favorite treat**: Crystallized pineapple
LEGO set: LEGO® Harry Potter™ Exclusive Set (5005254)

SCHOOL LIFE

During the day, studious young witches and wizards enjoy
learning new magical skills. Here, Hermione and Seamus
are trying out a levitation charm. After class, there's more
fun to be had, including Quidditch practice and delicious
feasts in the Great Hall. Sometimes a duel even breaks out!
Then there are the castle's many hidden secrets ...

POTIONS LESSON

The place to learn the **subtle science** and **exact art** of potion-making.

*I*n Potions class, students learn to brew amazing magical concoctions such as Sleeping Draughts, Love Potions, and Liquid Luck. Whenever a Potions class is in progress, Professor Snape's classroom fills with smoke, bubbles, and a variety of smells. Not all of the smells are pleasant!

In the Hogwarts Whomping Willow set, the students cook up their potions at the classroom table. Hermione Granger always follows Snape's instructions to the letter. The shocked-looking Seamus Finnigan minifigure has not been so careful. This accident-prone Gryffindor has a habit of causing chaos in the classroom. His cauldron is about to explode green goo all over his school uniform!

LEGO set: Hogwarts™ Whomping Willow™ (75953)

FLYING LESSONS

Fledgling flyers must learn **balance**, **control**, and a head for **heights**.

New students at Hogwarts begin flying classes with Madam Hooch in their very first week. No young witch or wizard will get far unless they master this essential skill.

These Harry Potter and Susan Bones minifigures soar above the pointed spires of the LEGO® Hogwarts Great Hall set, Harry on a brown broom and Susan on a black one. The minifigures grip their brooms with one hand—a risky flying maneuver! Harry has also brought his wand in case he needs to practice spell-casting while airborne.

Students from all houses take part in flying lessons together. Harry wears his Gryffindor uniform and Susan is in her Hufflepuff colors. They had better not fly too far, though, or they might miss the feast in the Great Hall below them.

LEGO set: Hogwarts™ Great Hall (75954)

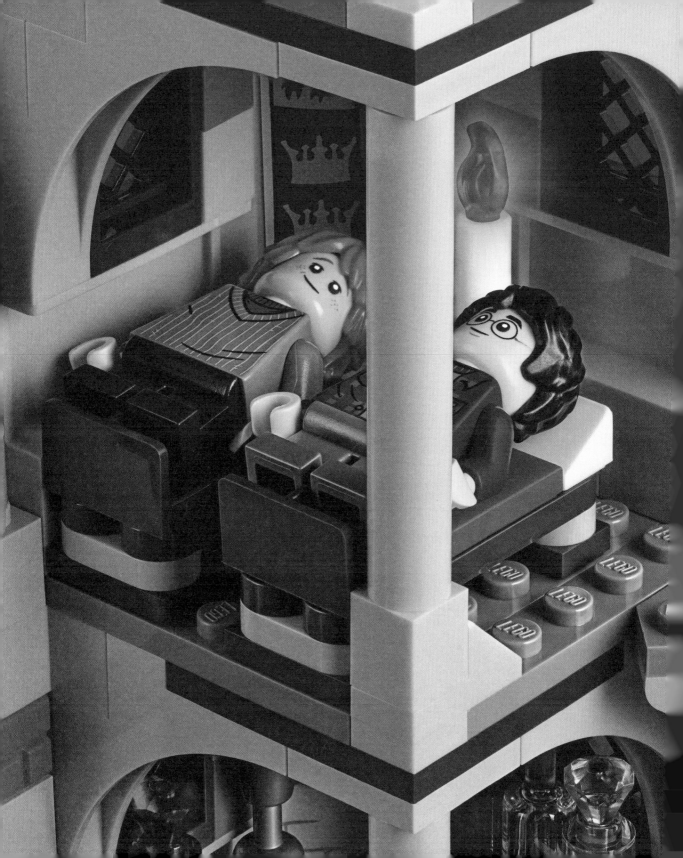

GRYFFINDOR DORMITORY

A **cozy, candlelit** space where students can **relax.**

*A*t Hogwarts, each house has dormitories where the students sleep. Harry and Ron share a dormitory. It has a low, arched ceiling and is lit by a candle. It is decorated with a Gryffindor banner.

Here, the Harry and Ron minifigures lie awake chatting in their dormitory. They crashed a car into the Whomping Willow earlier, so there is a lot to talk about! Their beds are side by side, with sloped white LEGO pieces for pillows. The Whomping Willow lies beyond the arched windows with their latticed shutters. Below the dormitory is the Potions classroom with its gleaming bottles stacked neatly away on shelves.

LEGO set: Hogwarts™ Whomping Willow™ (75953)

NEVILLE LONGBOTTOM

A **shy but brave** Gryffindor with a **talent** for Herbology.

Neville was raised by his grandmother. Now that he is at Hogwarts, this shy Gryffindor sometimes lacks confidence in his magical abilities. However, he excels at Herbology, the study of magical plants and fungi.

This Neville minifigure is wearing the school Herbology uniform of a protective beige overcoat. He wears brown gloves on his minifigure hands, ready to handle magical plants. This Herbology lesson is about Mandrakes, strange and dangerous plants whose root looks like a small creature. Neville wears earmuffs to protect his ears from the screeching cry of the Mandrake. This LEGO accessory is designed so that the Mandrake can be pulled out of the pot, revealing its angry face.

House: Gryffindor **Animal companion:** Trevor the toad
LEGO set: LEGO® Minifigures (71022)

DEAN THOMAS

Sports-mad student and a loyal friend.

Londoner Dean Thomas grew up in the Muggle world before receiving his invitation to Hogwarts. Like Harry, the Wizarding World is all new to Dean!

Sports-loving Dean is a huge soccer fan, but he didn't hear about Quidditch until arriving at Hogwarts. This Dean minifigure is dressed to attend a school Quidditch match. He is ready to cheer on his house, wrapped up in his Gryffindor scarf and waving a LEGO flag tile decorated with the Gryffindor colors and lion crest. His best friend is fellow Gryffindor Seamus Finnigan, and he gets on very well with Harry, Ron, and Hermione. Dean is a loyal Gryffindor, happy to support his friends in times of need.

House: Gryffindor **Best friend:** Seamus Finnigan
LEGO set: LEGO® Minifigures (71022)

THE OWLERY

The lofty, drafty, home of Hogwarts' faithful owl messengers.

*A*t the very top of Hogwarts West Tower is a round room built from stone. Glassless windows leave it open to the elements, and chilly drafts often blow through it. This is the Owlery—the place where the owls of Hogwarts live.

In the LEGO Hogwarts Whomping Willow set, Harry's snowy owl, Hedwig, is perched in the tower's tall, cone-shaped turret. She has shed a single loose feather. Many of the Owlery's residents are the school's messenger owls. Students and teachers use them to send and receive letters and parcels from home and beyond. The messenger owls share their accommodation with the owls brought to school by students. Hedwig might soon be joined by other owls of all colors and sizes.

LEGO set: Hogwarts™ Whomping Willow™ (75953)

MEALTIMES AT HOGWARTS

A time to **relax** and enjoy **delicious food** with classmates.

Meals are special occasions at Hogwarts. The whole school comes together to forget lessons, catch up with friends, and fill up on mouth-watering dishes.

The LEGO Hogwarts Great Hall set has long tables and benches where the students can all sit together to eat. Any students coming to dinner straight from Quidditch practice can hang up their brooms using the hooks on either side of the Great Hall's large front doors.

Susan Bones is calmly sipping her pumpkin juice at one of the tables. Ron does not look so calm. He has dropped his dessert on the floor and now Scabbers is heading straight for it. Scabbers's sweet tooth is even bigger than Ron's. Ron has to rescue his cake quickly!

LEGO set: Hogwarts™ Great Hall (75954)

THE MIRROR
OF ERISED

A **magical object** that reflects what your **heart most longs for**.

*T*his mirror's golden frame is engraved with the word "Erised"— "Desire" spelled backward. This is because the mirror reflects what you would most like to see. For Harry, whose parents died when he was a baby, his biggest wish is to be with them. When he looks in the mirror, he sees himself with his mom and dad, Lily and James Potter.

The Mirror of Erised can be found in the LEGO Great Hall model. It stands on a plinth, held between two ornate scroll bricks. The mirror's panels can be swapped to reflect the desires of different minifigures. As well as Harry with his parents, the mirror can also reflect Ron as Head Boy and Quidditch captain, Dumbledore holding a pair of cozy socks, or Professor Quirrell grasping the Sorcerer's Stone.

LEGO set: Hogwarts™ Great Hall (75954)

THE WHOMPING WILLOW

A **dangerous** tree that **lashes out** with the force of a **charging bull.**

The Whomping Willow is a magical tree growing in the grounds of Hogwarts. Beware this willow—it attacks anything that comes within reach of its spinning branches!

The gnarled branches of the LEGO Whomping Willow are all movable. They are made from angled LEGO® Technic elements and curved pieces, usually used for animal parts such as tails, tentacles, and elephant trunks. To recreate the tree's "whomping" action, the upper section can be spun at the turn of a dial, its branches lashing out as it goes around. At the base of the tree is a hole—is it the entrance to the secret tunnel leading to the Shrieking Shack?

Ron and Harry crash Arthur Weasley's flying Ford Anglia car into the Whomping Willow. They are soon flung out by the tree's spinning branches.

LEGO set: Hogwarts™ Whomping Willow (75953)

THE
DUELING CLUB

An **after-school** club where students train to repel **Dark Arts** attacks.

The Dueling Club is meant to teach students to defend themselves against the Dark Arts. In this meeting in Hogwarts Great Hall, Draco and Harry are more concerned with defending themselves against each other!

The two go head-to-head, brandishing their wands like swords. Tempers lost, they've forgotten the rules and are firing off spells way beyond the basic ones they should be using. Both minifigures' double-sided heads are turned to their fired-up expressions.

The Dueling Club was started when a Basilisk—also part of this set—was loose in the school. With things so out of hand, it could be time to break up the club (but not the Great Hall, which can be used for many other LEGO scenes!)

LEGO set: Hogwarts™ Great Hall (75954)

POLYJUICE POTION

A liquid concoction that transforms your appearance into that of someone else.

Brewing Polyjuice Potion requires advanced skills. That's why its recipe is kept in the Restricted Section of the school library. Smart Hermione has the skills, but not some of the ingredients—they are forbidden to students.

In the LEGO Hogwarts Great Hall set, Hermione's minifigure creeps up the movable spiral staircase to the Potions classroom in the round tower. There, she can take what she needs from Professor Snape's personal supplies.

Now Hermione just needs a few other ingredients to brew the potion: time, patience, and magical skill. Soon, she will be able to impersonate any of the nine other minifigures in this set—perfect for exploring the castle in disguise!

LEGO set: Hogwarts™ Great Hall (75954)

NEARLY HEADLESS NICK

The friendly **resident ghost** of **Gryffindor Tower.**

Sir Nicholas de Mimsy-Porpington is one of the ghosts that live at Hogwarts. Known as Nearly Headless Nick, he is a little sensitive about not being completely headless like some other, more intimidating ghosts.

However, Nick has his wish come true in the LEGO Great Hall set. His deathly white head comes right off! It even clips onto his minifigure hand so that he can carry it while he floats around. Nick's face is printed with an elegant mustache and beard for a refined appearance. He wears the fancy clothes of a fifteenth-century knight: tights, breeches, and a fashionable embroidered doublet. Well, it was fashionable in his own times! They're all in shades of ghostly gray, with shimmery silver printing.

House: Gryffindor **Ambition:** To join the Headless Hunt
LEGO set: Hogwarts™ Great Hall (75954)

QUIDDITCH MATCH

A thrilling, **high-flying** sport played by two teams on **broomsticks**.

*F*or many Hogwarts students, the highlight of the year is the annual Quidditch Tournament, in which the houses compete for the Quidditch Cup. In his scarlet robes, this Harry Potter minifigure is the star of the Gryffindor team. As the Seeker, it is his job to catch the tiny Golden Snitch.

In this match, Gryffindor goes head to head with their arch rivals, Slytherin. Harry has a face of concentration while he looks for the Snitch. His teammate Oliver Wood can be moved with a lever to defend the Gryffindor goal hoops from Slytherin Chaser Marcus Flint. Meanwhile, Lucian Bole, the Slytherin Beater, is armed with a bat to aim black Bludgers toward the Gryffindor players. Bole's alarmed face suggests he's seen that Harry has almost reached the Snitch! Will Harry catch it and win Gryffindor the match?

LEGO set: Quidditch™ Match (75956)

CHO CHANG

A **smart** and **sensitive** Ravenclaw student.

*C*lever young witch Cho is a popular member of Ravenclaw house. She attends the Yule Ball with Cedric Diggory in her fifth year. Cho has a rebellious streak—in her sixth year, she joins Dumbledore's Army, a secret club where students meet to practice defensive spells.

This Cho minifigure has long, black hair and a calm smile. Her Ravenclaw tie is neatly knotted. She has borrowed a Hogwarts owl from the Owlery, because she has no owl of her own. She has chosen a large, tan-and-cream bird— perfect for sending a birthday present or a letter. Cho carries her wand, ready to conjure up a charm if necessary!

House: Ravenclaw **Patronus:** Swan
LEGO set: LEGO® Minifigures (71022)

CEDRIC DIGGORY

A **popular** student, a **sporting** hero, and a worthy **champion** of Hogwarts.

Brave but modest, competitive but fair, Cedric Diggory is one of Hogwarts' most popular boys. He is captain of the Hufflepuff Quidditch team and a much-liked prefect.

This Cedric minifigure is competing in the Triwizard Tournament, a contest between Europe's three major wizarding schools. Chosen as Hogwarts' champion, Cedric competes against rivals from Beauxbatons Academy of Magic and the Durmstrang Institute. He must complete three tasks, including finding the Triwizard Cup in a magical maze. His minifigure wears competitors' clothes in the colors of his house, with his name printed on the back. With his Hogwarts badge shining on his chest, Cedric looks every inch the heroic school champion.

House: Hufflepuff   **Quidditch position:** Seeker
LEGO set: LEGO® Minifigures (71022)

INVISIBILITY CLOAK

A magical cape that completely conceals the person under it.

Harry receives an anonymous gift one Christmas—an Invisibility Cloak! It's one of a kind and a very rare object. When tucked around Harry's neck, his body completely disappears. If Harry doesn't cover his head, it looks as if his head is floating in midair—spooky!

Here, Harry is in pajamas and bare feet because he mostly uses the cloak for roaming around Hogwarts at night, when his fellow students are asleep. His ruffled hair looks like he just got out of bed. But this hairpiece is on seven other Harry minifigures—that's just the way his messy hair always is! The cape is made of iridescent material, with a magical pattern of swirling spirals and stars on the inside.

LEGO set: LEGO® Minifigures (71022)

A DRESSING DOWN

"You were seen! By no less than seven Muggles!"

It's forbidden for students to use magic outside school—and doubly bad to be seen by Muggles when doing so. In the Hogwarts Whomping Willow set, Ron and Harry have a dangerous run-in when they crash a flying car into the violent Whomping Willow. But things go from bad to worse when they're sent to Professor Snape's office. The set includes Snape's dingy office, full of potion ingredients.

Instead of having their smiles on show, Harry and Ron's double-sided LEGO minifigure faces are turned to look very worried. Not only did they come to school in a reckless and illegal way, their magic was seen by Muggles. Their strange behavior is all over the newspapers. Snape looks furious! What punishment will he dish out?

LEGO set: Hogwarts™ Whomping Willow™ (75953)

ARGUS FILCH

The **cranky caretaker** of Hogwarts who **delights** in getting students into trouble.

Unpleasant Argus Filch works in a school even though he doesn't seem to like the students. He is a Squib, which means that he comes from a magical family, but has no magical ability himself. Filch loves catching students who are up to no good, and enjoys dishing out punishments.

The thin gray hair of Filch's minifigure is connected to the bald-patch element that clips onto his head. He wears a mold-colored waistcoat, a creased shirt, and a bedraggled tie. His face is printed with saggy jowls and sideburns. As a Squib, the caretaker has no magical accessories, but he holds a torch for nighttime patrols and carries keys to unlock the many mysterious doors of the castle.

House: None **Animal companion:** Mrs. Norris the cat
LEGO set: Hogwarts™ Whomping Willow™ (75953)

DRACO MALFOY

A **rich** and **arrogant** Slytherin student and Harry's **arch-rival.**

Draco Malfoy's father is a powerful, snobbish wizard. He raised Draco to look down on anyone poor or not from a pure-blood wizard family. No wonder Draco turned into a smug bully and was sorted straight into Slytherin house!

When Draco isn't bullying classmates or trying to impress important adults, he practices his Quidditch skills. Like Harry, Draco plays as Seeker for his house team. He must chase the Golden Snitch: the tiny, winged ball that zips around the Quidditch field. All set to play, Draco's minifigure has a green tunic with a Slytherin crest, a short green cape, brown flying gloves, white pants, and clutches a pearl-gold Snitch. His trademark smirking face looks a little unsettled here. Maybe he is worried his team will lose to Gryffindor!

House: Slytherin **Skills:** Flying **Parents:** Lucius and Narcissa Malfoy
LEGO set: LEGO® Minifigures (71022)

LUNA LOVEGOOD

A **dreamy, quirky** Ravenclaw who's not afraid to **be herself.**

Whimsical Luna likes to do things in her own unique way. She is a thoughtful friend and an artistic, talented student. Not one to follow mainstream fashions, her colorful minifigure wears a bright-pink top printed with pockets and pleats. Her skirt is patterned with cosmic stars, moons, hearts, horses, and birds. Whatever she keeps in the bag slung across her body is likely to be unusual. Perhaps a pair of magical Spectrespecs or a Butterbeer-cork necklace!

Luna's minifigure carries a *Quibbler* newspaper tile. *The Quibbler* is often full of far-fetched stories and conspiracy theories. This copy reports that there is "pandemonium at the Ministry." Could the stories be true? Luna should know, as the paper is edited by her father!

House: Ravenclaw **Patronus:** Hare **Favorite earrings:** Radishes
LEGO set: LEGO® Minifigures (71022)

DEFENSE AGAINST THE DARK ARTS

The wizarding world has wonderful things to offer, but as Hagrid tells Harry, not all wizards are good. To prepare students for danger, Hogwarts teaches Defense Against the Dark Arts. During Harry's time at Hogwarts, he has several different Defense Against the Dark Arts teachers. They never seem to last more than one year in the job!

LORD VOLDEMORT

The most powerful Dark wizard, known as
He Who Must Not Be Named.

*L*ord Voldemort is the most feared Dark wizard of all time. Many people in the magical community do not even like to say his name. He is usually referred to as He Who Must Not Be Named, or You-Know-Who.

Not completely human, he has deathly white skin, orange eyes, and snakelike features. He looks nothing like the promising Slytherin schoolboy he used to be, when he went by the name Tom Marvolo Riddle.

The minifigure who must not be named wears simple, long, green robes—all the better for achieving world domination. He always keeps his faithful snake, Nagini, close by. She is more than a pet—she contains a part of Voldemort's soul!

House: Slytherin **Animal companion:** Nagini the snake **Skills:** Speaking Parseltongue (snake language) **LEGO set:** LEGO® Minifigures (71022)

THE DREADED DEMENTORS

Sinister, gliding creatures who guard Azkaban prison.

*T*he hooded Dementors are terrifying creatures. They feed on human happiness, draining all hope from their victims. The worst fate of all is the Dementor's Kiss, during which they suck out a person's soul.

At the start of Harry's third year, Dementors board the train in search of an escaped prisoner, so a Dementor is included in the Hogwarts Express set. LEGO® Dementors are similar to minifigures, but instead of legs they have a stand that appears to melt away into smoke. Their torso is printed with an exposed ribcage, and they wear ragged cloaks. Dementors cannot see, so their heads have no eyes, but they do have mouths—pursed to give a Dementor's Kiss. To defeat one, try to think the happiest thoughts you can!

LEGO set: Hogwarts™ Express (75955)

MAD-EYE MOODY

A blunt, battle-scarred Auror with a watchful magical eye.

*A*lastor Moody comes from a long line of Aurors—official law-enforcers of the wizarding world. This tough-talking wizard has suffered many injuries in battles against the Dark Arts. He now stomps along on a false leg and wears a magical eye that has earned him his nickname: "Mad-Eye."

This Mad-Eye Moody minifigure looks as if he is on the lookout for Dark Arts activity. His magical eye, strapped to his scarred face, sees in all directions. It can even see through things, including through the back of his own head! Moody has his staff and wand ready, in case of sudden attacks from Dark wizards.

Best fighting skill: Dueling **Characteristics:** Vigilance, boldness, and dedication **LEGO set:** LEGO® Minifigures (71022)

PROFESSOR LUPIN

A kind teacher dedicated to fighting evil, but who carries a **heavy burden**.

Bitten as a child by a werewolf, Remus Lupin grew up hiding a frightening secret. Every full moon he turns into an uncontrollable, monstrous werewolf. Luckily, Lupin has a network of friends who help him manage and hide his condition. Many in the wizarding world do not trust werewolves, but this hasn't upset kindhearted Lupin.

Harry Potter first meets this unusual teacher on the Hogwarts Express, and so Lupin's minifigure can be found in this set. Here, he is protecting Harry and his friends from the ghastly Dementor that has boarded the train looking for a runaway prisoner. Lupin doesn't like to draw attention, so his minifigure wears bland, beige and gray clothes. His face is printed with stubble, a mustache, and scars.

House: Gryffindor **Subject:** Defense Against the Dark Arts
Favorite food: Chocolate **LEGO set:** Hogwarts™ Express (75955)

DOLORES UMBRIDGE

A **sinister** Ministry official who wants **control of Hogwarts.**

Don't be fooled by this minifigure's harmless appearance. She may look sweet in her pink, frilly outfit, but she is actually a cruel and dangerous witch. The other side of her face reveals a fiercer expression! Dolores Umbridge arrives at Hogwarts from the Ministry of Magic and proves to be a harsh and unkind Defense Against the Dark Arts teacher. For a while she is even Headmistress, and enjoys inventing rules and punishing students just for fun.

Umbridge's minifigure is prim and proper in pink, from her tweed dress to her heeled shoes. Her hairpiece is perfectly styled and a cute kitten badge is pinned to her cardigan. She loves to collect dainty things, such as the pretty teacup she is holding here.

House: Slytherin **Subject:** Defense Against the Dark Arts **Patronus:** Cat
LEGO set: LEGO® Harry Potter™ Exclusive set (5005254)

PROFESSOR QUIRRELL

A **nervous** professor who is **not quite what he seems**.

Quirinus Quirrell has an excellent knowledge of Defense Against the Dark Arts, but he's not so good at putting it into practice. The intelligent professor is shy, shaky, and easily overruled.

Quirrell is Hogwarts' Defense Against the Dark Arts teacher in Harry's first year. Quirrell's minifigure sports a purple turban with the end of the fabric draped around his shoulders. The turban is a special LEGO mold, and the purple fabric is printed onto his torso, over his suit. Under the turban, Quirrell is hiding a double-sided head print. His other face looks suspiciously like that of a certain evil wizard who shall not be named!

House: Ravenclaw **Subject:** Defense Against the Dark Arts
Skill: Keeping secrets **LEGO set:** Hogwarts™ Great Hall (75954)

NEVILLE'S BOGGART

A magical creature that looks like
whatever scares you the most.

You can find all sorts of strange creatures in a Defense Against the Dark Arts classroom. A Boggart shape-shifts into the greatest fear of whoever is confronting it. This LEGO Boggart resembles Neville Longbottom's deepest dread: Professor Snape!

The trick to defeating a Boggart is to remove its power. The incantation *Riddikulus!* combined with laughter usually does the trick. To laugh, make the Boggart look silly—this could be by imagining roller skates on an Acromantula or picturing Snape in Neville's grandmother's clothes.

Therefore, this Snape-like Boggart minifigure wears Mrs. Longbottom's clothes, with a black hat; a large, crimson handbag; and a fox-fur stole. Snape, or perhaps the Boggart, does not look amused.

LEGO set: LEGO® Harry Potter™ Exclusive Set (5005254)

THE DEADLY BASILISK

Underneath Hogwarts lurks an enormous secret serpent that kills at first glance.

Never look a Basilisk in the eye. Its stare kills instantly. If seen in the reflection of a puddle or mirror, or even through a camera or a ghost, then this sinister creature will merely Petrify, freezing its victim to the spot.

The king of serpents lives in the Chamber of Secrets—a hidden room in Hogwarts that's opened during Harry's second year. This huge snake is longer than four standard LEGO minifigures and can hold a minifigure easily in its hinged jaws. Constructed around five ball-and-socket joints, the horned reptile can be twisted into different positions. Here, it rears up on its thick tail, ready to strike. Once the Basilisk is defeated, its fangs clip out easily. Take care, though—a Basilisk's teeth contain venom!

Powers: Fatal stare **Controlled by:** Salazar Slytherin and his descendants, including Tom Riddle. **LEGO set:** Hogwarts™ Great Hall (7̶̶854)

MAGICAL CREATURES

A fantastic array of magical creatures can be found at Hogwarts and beyond. Some are great animal companions. Some produce special magic, such as a phoenix's healing tears. Some do useful work, like house-elves and the owls who deliver the mail. Others, like the eight-legged Acromantula, are best avoided.

FAWKES THE PHOENIX

Dumbledore's **loyal phoenix,** with a **never-ending** life cycle.

Fawkes the phoenix has special powers. When he comes to the end of his life cycle, he bursts into flames and is then reborn as a tiny chick from the fire's ashes. This event is known as Burning Day. In *Harry Potter and the Chamber of Secrets*, Harry gets a shock the first time he sees it!

Fawkes is loyal to his master, Professor Dumbledore. He lives in Dumbledore's office and often comes to the aid of those who need magical help. His feathers are scarlet and gold—just like the colors of Dumbledore's house, Gryffindor.

Despite their small size, phoenixes can lift incredibly heavy loads. In the Hogwarts Great Hall set, Fawkes has a clip piece for claws that can also attach to LEGO® builds for carrying. He is formed around a 1x1 brick with studs on all sides. His orange wings are a new element made especially for Fawkes. A red horn piece clips onto his head for a plume.

Breed: Phoenix **Powers:** Healing tears, carrying heavy loads, rebirth
LEGO set: Hogwarts™ Great Hall (75954)

MAGICAL COMPANIONS

Hogwarts students are allowed to keep animals at school.

The summer before Harry starts at Hogwarts, Hagrid buys him a birthday gift: a snowy owl named Hedwig. Harry's loyal companion has gray feather details and yellow-and-black eyes. In the LEGO® Minifigures series, she perches primly on Harry's hand.

An old rat with a bald patch on his head isn't Ron's idea of a perfect pet—but he loves Scabbers all the same. Scabbers belonged to Ron's older brother Percy and has been in the Weasley family for years.

Hermione's large ginger cat, Crookshanks, is intelligent and perceptive, just like his owner. He thinks there's something suspicious about Scabbers. If only Crookshanks could talk!

LEGO set: LEGO® Minifigures (71022)

DOBBY THE HOUSE-ELF

Hard-working and humble, this house-elf is now a free elf!

Bat-eared Dobby is a little house-elf who works hard in the service of the Malfoy family. His cruel masters make life miserable for him.

This Dobby minifigure has just won his freedom—thanks to Harry Potter. Clever Harry tricked Lucius Malfoy into handing a sock to Dobby, hidden inside Tom Riddle's diary. The LEGO sock tile fits neatly inside the hinged, black book. In the magical world, a house-elf is freed if his master gives him clothes. Here, Dobby sports the dirty pillowcase he wears at Malfoy Manor. After being freed he gets some proper clothes, and remains especially fond of socks!

Dobby is a loyal friend and magical helper to Harry forevermore, always calling him by his full name, Harry Potter, and often respectfully adding "Sir."

Magical skills: Ability to perform magic without a wand
LEGO set: LEGO® Minifigures (71022)

ARAGOG THE ACROMANTULA

A **giant, flesh-eating** spider that can **talk.**

Deep in the Forbidden Forest dwells Aragog. He is a magical breed of giant spider called an Acromantula. Aragog is friendly to Hagrid, but all other humans are just potential dinner to him.

In the Aragog's Lair set, Harry and Ron are exploring the forest with a lantern and torch when they stumble into the spider's den. Now they are face to face with Aragog, with his huge staring eyes and movable fangs. As well as avoiding Aragog's fangs, Harry and Ron should watch out for that tree—it shoots LEGO spider webs!

Aragog's spider children scuttle all around the lair. This isn't very good for Ron's spider phobia, as his scared minifigure face clearly shows!

Birthplace: A distant land **Diet:** Meat—preferably human
Number of fangs: Four **LEGO set:** Aragog's Lair (75950)

INDEX

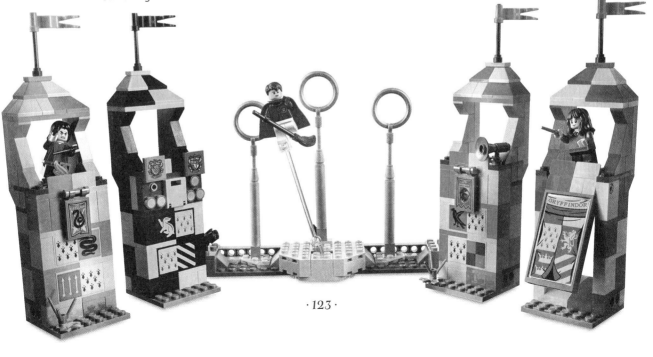

Written by Elizabeth Dowsett, Julia March,
and Rosie Peet
Edited by Rosie Peet and Emma Grange
Designed by Lisa Robb and James McKeag
Senior Pre-Production Producer Jen Murray
Senior Producer Louise Daly
Managing Editor Paula Regan
Managing Art Editor Jo Connor
Publisher Julie Ferris
Art Director Lisa Lanzarini
Publishing Director Simon Beecroft

Dorling Kindersley would like to thank
Randi K. Sørensen, Heidi K. Jensen, Paul Hansford,
and Martin Leighton Lindhard at the LEGO Group;
Victoria Selover and Katie Campbell at Warner Bros.
Consumer Products; Megan Douglass for
proofreading; Helen Peters for writing the index,
and Nicole Reynolds for editorial assistance.

First American Edition, 2019
Published in the United States by DK Publishing,1450 Broadway, Suite 801,
New York, NY 10018

Page design copyright © 2019 Dorling Kindersley Limited
DK, a Division of Penguin Random House LLC
19 20 21 22 23 10 9 8 7 6 5 4 3 2 1
001–315507–Jul/2019

Copyright © 2019 Warner Bros. Entertainment Inc.
HARRY POTTER characters, names and related indicia are © &
™ Warner Bros. Entertainment Inc. WB SHIELD: © & ™ WBEI.
WIZARDING WORLD trademark and logo © & ™ Warner Bros.
Entertainment Inc. Publishing Rights © & JKR. (s19)
DORL41983

LEGO, the LEGO logo, the Minifigure and the Brick and Knob
configurations are trademarks and/or copyrights of the LEGO Group.
All rights reserved. ©2019 The LEGO Group.

Manufactured by Dorling Kindersley, 80 Strand, London, WC2R 0RL, UK,
under license from the LEGO Group.

All rights reserved. Without limiting the rights under the copyright reserved
above, no part of this publication may be reproduced, stored in or introduced
into a retrieval system, or transmitted, in any form, or by any means
(electronic, mechanical, photocopying, recording, or otherwise),
without the prior written permission of the copyright owner.

Published in Great Britain by Dorling Kindersley Limited.

A catalog record for this book is available
from the Library of Congress.

ISBN 978-1-4654-8766-7

DK books are available at special discounts when purchased in bulk
for sales promotions, premiums, fund-raising, or educational use.
For details, contact: DK Publishing Special Markets,
1450 Broadway, Suite 801, New York, NY 10018
SpecialSales@dk.com

Printed and bound in China

www.lego.com
www.dk.com

A WORLD OF IDEAS:
SEE ALL THERE IS TO KNOW